FOREWORD

This first adventure of Tintin, the boy reporter, appeared in 1929 in a children's supplement to a Belgian daily newspaper, *Le Vingtième Siècle*. Hergé, Georges Remi, then twenty-two years old, was employed on the staff as an artist. He had received no formal art training, but was already showing the originality and wit that would make him a unique figure in the world of the strip cartoon.

Hergé's satire on the Soviet state was very much of its time. He himself had not been to Russia, but had read a book published the year before, *Moscou sans voiles: Neuf ans de travail au pays des Soviets* by Joseph Douillet, a former Belgian consul in Rostov-on-Don. Soviet propaganda to persuade the world outside Russia that the economy was booming was a particular target for Hergé, as were the activities of the secret police, the OGPU. Incidentally, he errs on one occasion in the story when he calls them the Cheka, their name before 1922.

Publication of *Le Petit Vingtième* began on 10 January 1929. In 1930 the adventure was issued in album form, now a very rare book greatly sought after, the 500 copies being numbered and signed "Tintin et Milou". There were, it is believed, nine subsequent editions, differing only in the layout of the print on the title page. With the exception of a reissue in 1969 for the personal use of the author, again limited to 500 copies, and some pirated editions, more than forty years elapsed before this adventure was again published, in the first volume of the *Archives Hergé*.

L. L-C   M. T.

TRANSLATED BY
LESLIE LONSDALE-COOPER AND MICHAEL TURNER

The TINTIN books are published in the following languages:

Alsacien	CASTERMAN		Indonesian	INDIRA
Basque	ELKAR		Italian	CASTERMAN
Bengali	ANANDA		Japanese	FUKUINKAN
Bernese	EMMENTALER DRUCK		Korean	CASTERMAN/SOL
Breton	AN HERE		Latin	ELI/CASTERMAN
Catalan	CASTERMAN		Luxembourgeois	IMPRIMERIE SAINT-PAUL
Chinese	CASTERMAN/CHINA CHILDREN PUBLISHING		Norwegian	EGMONT
Corsican	CASTERMAN		Picard	CASTERMAN
Danish	CARLSEN		Polish	CASTERMAN/MOTOPOL
Dutch	CASTERMAN		Portuguese	CASTERMAN
English	EGMONT BOOKS LTD/LITTLE, BROWN & CO.		Provençal	CASTERMAN
Esperanto	ESPERANTIX/CASTERMAN		Romanche	LIGIA ROMONTSCHA
Finnish	OTAVA		Russian	CASTERMAN
French	CASTERMAN		Serbo-Croatian	DECJE NOVINE
Gallo	RUE DES SCRIBES		Spanish	CASTERMAN
Gaumais	CASTERMAN		Swedish	CARLSEN
German	CARLSEN		Thai	CASTERMAN
Greek	CASTERMAN		Tibetan	CASTERMAN
Hebrew	MIZRAHI		Turkish	YAPI KREDI YAYINLARI

EGMONT
We bring stories to life

Artwork copyright © by Editions Casterman, Paris and Tournai
Text copyright © 1999 Casterman/Moulinsart
First published in Great Britain in 1999 by Egmont UK Limited,
Hardback edition published in 2009 and paperback edition published in 2014 by
Egmont UK Limited, The Yellow Building, 1 Nicholas Road, London, W11 4AN
A CIP catalogue record for this title is available from the British Library.

Hardback: ISBN 978 1 4052 1477 3
Paperback: ISBN 978 1 4052 6651 2

THE ADVENTURES OF
T I N T I N
REPORTER FOR "LE PETIT VINGTIÈME"
IN THE LAND OF
THE SOVIETS

BY HERGÉ

EGMONT

AT "LE PETIT XXᴱ" WE ARE ALWAYS EAGER TO SATISFY OUR READERS AND KEEP THEM UP TO DATE ON FOREIGN AFFAIRS. WE HAVE THEREFORE SENT

TINTIN

ONE OF OUR TOP REPORTERS, TO SOVIET RUSSIA. EACH WEEK WE SHALL BE BRINGING YOU NEWS OF HIS MANY ADVENTURES.

N.B. THE EDITOR OF "LE PETIT XXᴱ" GUARANTEES THAT ALL PHOTOGRAPHS ARE ABSOLUTELY AUTHENTIC, TAKEN BY TINTIN HIMSELF, AIDED BY HIS FAITHFUL DOG SNOWY!

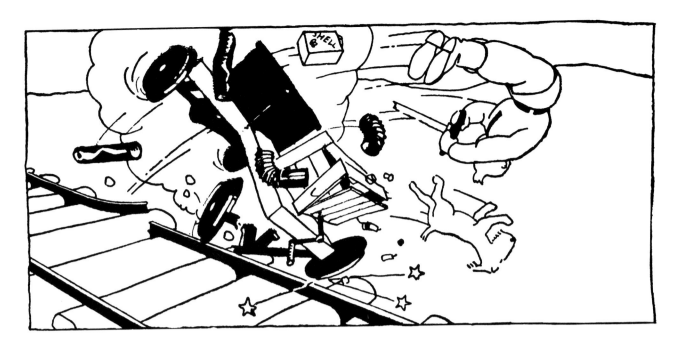

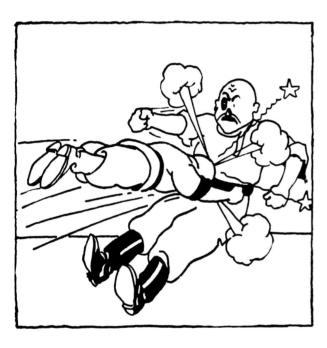

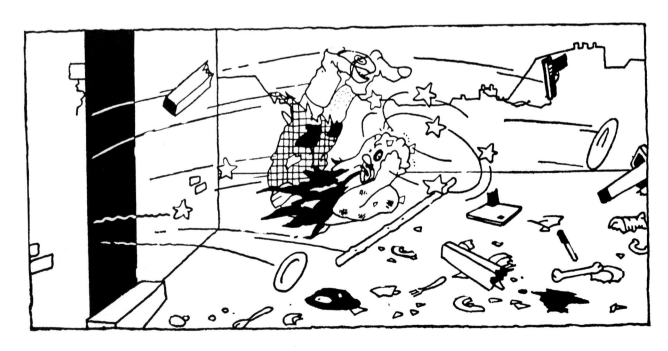

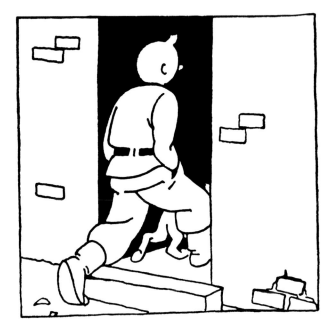

THERE, THAT'S DONE. BUT HOW CAN I GET THIS BACK TO THE OFFICE?

OH WELL, WE'LL THINK ABOUT THAT TOMORROW. NOW TO BED.

I'M GOING TO SLEEP IN MY CLOTHES... IT'S SAFER...

ZZZZZZ ZZZZZ ZZZZ ZZZZ

ZZZ..... ZZZ...... ZZZ......

SSH! YOU'LL WAKE HIM UP.

36

TO PINCH MY CAR FROM UNDER MY VERY NOSE! THAT'S THE LIMIT!

JUST YOU WAIT, MY FRIEND... A MATCH TO THIS TRICKLE OF PETROL...

... AND NOW, BON VOYAGE!

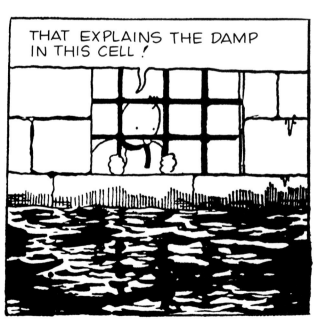

WHILE THEY DISEMBARK, I'LL TAKE ADVANTAGE OF THE CONFUSION AND GO TO THE VILLAGE. I'LL WARN THE INHABITANTS THEY ARE ABOUT TO BE ROBBED!

I MUST GET THE CORN HIDDEN, BEFORE THE SEARCH BY THE SOVIETS!

THE SOVIETS ARE COMING ...THEY'RE GOING TO STEAL YOUR GRAIN!

WHERE TO HIDE THE CORN ??

LUCKY FOR US, ON THE JOURNEY IN THE TRUCK I TOOK THE POWDER OUT OF THE CARTRIDGES AND REPLACED THE BULLETS WITH WADS OF CARDBOARD!

NOW, WE MUSTN'T HANG AROUND HERE... IT'S AN UNHEALTHY SPOT!

IT'S GETTING DARK, AND SNOW IS STARTING TO FALL...

WORSE TO COME!

TRAMPING IN THE SNOW IS EXHAUSTING.

OOF! I CAN'T GO ANY FURTHER... DO I HAVE TO DIE HERE?

THE OGPU MIGHT HAVE CHOSEN ANOTHER DAY TO SEND US OUT AFTER THAT JOURNALIST SPY, TINTIN!

I'M NOT GOING ON!

THAT'S O.K., WE'LL STOP.

?

LORD ALONE KNOWS WHERE TINTIN IS NOW.

NOT THE MOST AGREEABLE COMPANY! BETTER MAKE MYSELF SCARCE.

TINTIN!

TINTIN!

-HERGÉ-

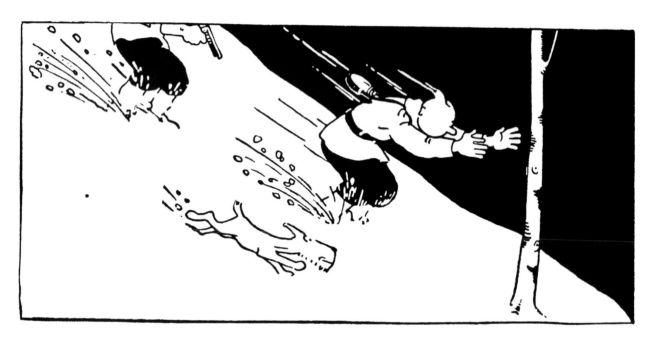

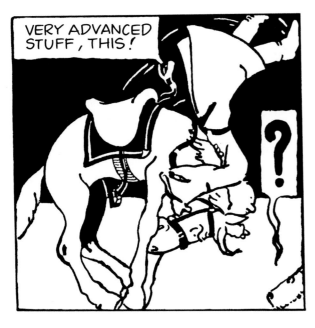

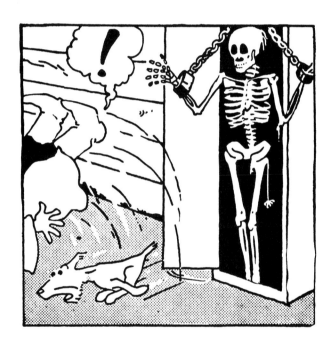

TAKE HIM TO OUR LEADER!

TIE HIM SECURELY, AND LEAVE US. I WANT TO TALK TO HIM.

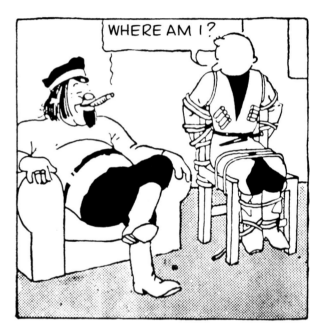

WHERE AM I?

YOU'RE IN THE HIDEOUT WHERE LENIN, TROTSKY AND STALIN HAVE COLLECTED TOGETHER WEALTH STOLEN FROM THE PEOPLE! ALL AROUND THIS PLACE ARE IMMENSE, EMPTY STEPPES, ALMOST IMPASSABLE. BUT IF BY CHANCE A PEASANT WANDERED INTO THE HAUNTED ROOM WHICH COVERS THE ENTRANCE TO OUR VAULTS, HE'D BE FAR TOO SCARED TO PURSUE HIS INVESTIGATIONS.

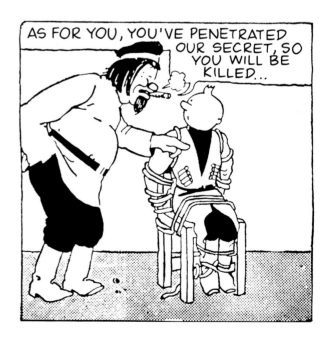

AS FOR YOU, YOU'VE PENETRATED OUR SECRET, SO YOU WILL BE KILLED...

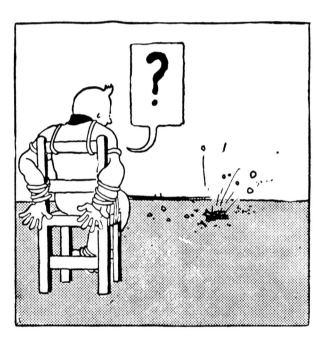

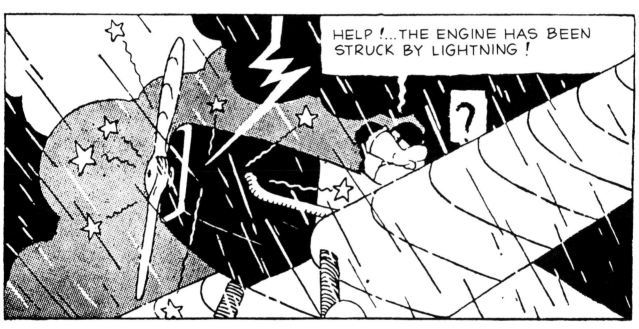

OH! THE PLANE IS GOING TO SMASH INTO THAT FACTORY CHIMNEY!

YET ANOTHER BRUSH WITH DEATH!

HAVE YOU QUITE FINISHED YOUR ACROBATICS?...

THAT'S REPAIRED THE FUEL TANK.

IT REALLY IS TOO BAD, TINTIN, CLOWNING AROUND LIKE THAT AT YOUR AGE!

PHEW... SAVED!

HELLO! AN AERODROME!

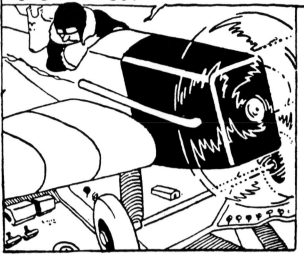

I DON'T UNDERSTAND !... ALTHOUGH I'M ALL DISGUISED AS A TIGER THEY DON'T SEEM THE LEAST BIT BOTHERED !

HERGE

THE BOLSHEVIK WHO COLLAPSED AT THE SIGHT OF THE TIGER CAME ROUND. INSTEAD OF EXECUTING ME, HE LEFT ME HERE, CONDEMNING ME TO DEATH BY STARVATION.

LUCKY THE IDIOT FORGOT TO TAKE HIS KEYS!

ALL RIGHT?...

YES...

FREE!... FREE!...

THANKS TO ME!

BERLIN 15 KM

THREE HOURS' WALK!... THAT'S NOTHING FOR US!

AND THEN WE GO HOME?...

COURAGE, SNOWY!

YES, BUT I'M TERRIBLY THIRSTY.

BERLIN!

AT LAST! NOW TO EAT AND DRINK AND SLEEP.

·HERGÉ